My Perfect Wedding

By Lisa Ann Marsoli

$\mathcal{C}$inderella's dreams were coming true at last! She and the Prince were going to be married, and a new life filled with happiness would soon begin.

But first, there was a wedding to plan. . . .

Prudence, Cinderella's lady-in-waiting, was in charge of the planning. She had a very long list of tasks.

"Excuse me," Cinderella asked Prudence, "couldn't we just have a simple wedding?"

Prudence frowned. "Cinderella, now that you are going to be a princess, you must start thinking big!"

Later, Prudence arrived with the royal dressmaker and several wedding gowns.

"Do you think you can design something . . . plainer?" Cinderella asked politely.

"Certainly not!" Prudence said. "*Plain* and *princess* do not go together!"

Next it was time to select the flowers. The florist greeted them with . . . a rosebush!

"Do you have something a bit . . . smaller?" Cinderella asked.

"This is perfect," Prudence said. "You just have to know how to carry it." Prudence held the flowers out in front of her and—*buzzzz*—she was stung by a bee!

"Prudence has gone to bed to nurse her bee sting. I'll have to plan the wedding myself," Cinderella said to the mice. "Now, what should I do first?"

"Who's-a comin', Cinderelly?" asked Jaq.

"The guest list! Good idea, Jaq. Well, of course all of you are invited," Cinderella replied. "And my fairy godmother . . . I wish she were here right now."

Suddenly, a twinkling light filled the room, and Cinderella's fairy godmother appeared! "We'll plan an absolutely magical wedding for you, my dear," she said, giving Cinderella a big hug. "Now, when is it exactly?"

Gus counted on his fingers. "Tomorrow!" he announced.

"Oh, my goodness, child!" cried the Fairy Godmother.

"Lots ta do!" Jaq added.

"Well, then, let's start at the beginning—with the dress!" the Fairy Godmother said. She waved her wand, and Cinderella found herself in an elegant white gown. But her fairy godmother had forgotten the veil.

"It's lovely," Cinderella said, "but don't you think it needs . . . ?"

The Fairy Godmother wasn't listening. She was already working on the next task—invitations! In moments, hundreds of lovely pink cards sat in stacks around the room.

"Now we shall prepare the feast and make the cake!" she announced.

Cinderella changed out of her gown and followed her fairy godmother to the royal kitchen. The mice picked up where the Fairy Godmother had left off. Mary, Suzy, and Perla pulled out a box of tiny pearls and began making a veil.

And Jaq gave each of the other mice an armload of invitations to deliver. Unfortunately, they didn't get very far before Pom-Pom the cat showed up!

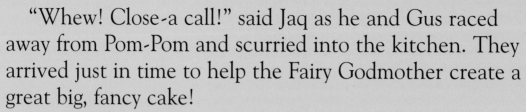

"Whew! Close-a call!" said Jaq as he and Gus raced away from Pom-Pom and scurried into the kitchen. They arrived just in time to help the Fairy Godmother create a great big, fancy cake!

Cinderella tried to hide her disappointment. "Um . . . Prudence will love it," she said. "You know, I really should see how she's feeling."

"Poor child," the Fairy Godmother said after Cinderella
had left. "These wedding plans must be too much for her."
Jaq and Gus tugged at the Fairy Godmother's sleeve.
"Cinderelly likes smaller things," Jaq told her. "Like mice!"
All at once, the Fairy Godmother understood.

Later, the Fairy Godmother took Cinderella's hand.
"I'm afraid I may have gotten a bit carried away, my dear,"
the Fairy Godmother confessed. "Now, tell me, child, what
would the wedding of your dreams be like?"

23

After listening to Cinderella, the Fairy Godmother finished the beautiful veil. Then she got rid of all the invitations by magically sending them to destinations near and far.

"Now let's cut that cake down to size," the Fairy Godmother said.

As they left for the kitchen, Cinderella turned toward the kindhearted mice. "Thank you, my little friends," she said gratefully.

The next day, Cinderella looked lovely in her simple white gown, veil, and gloves. But something was missing.

"Good heavens, child!" the Fairy Godmother exclaimed. "You can't get married in your bare feet!" She waved her wand, and Cinderella's beautiful glass slippers peeked out from underneath her gown.

After the ceremony, the Prince and Cinderella shared a joyous celebration with their guests. Even Prudence was pleased.

"However did you manage all of this?" the Prince asked his new princess.

Cinderella smiled and said, "With friends by your side, anything is possible!"

Two Hearts

By Catherine McCafferty

One day, Snow
White decided to visit her
friends the Seven Dwarfs.

"I'll be back soon, dear," Snow White said
as she leaned down to kiss the Prince.

Snow White couldn't believe how much her life had changed.
The evil Queen was gone, and she was married to her prince. In
fact, they would celebrate their first anniversary the next day!

"Well, hello, Snow White!" cried the Dwarfs when she arrived at the cottage.

"Oh, I've missed you so!" said Snow White. "Why don't I make you some supper?"

As the Dwarfs ate their meal, Snow White asked for their help. "The Prince and I will celebrate our first anniversary tomorrow, and I want to make dinner for him here. Also, the Prince is very precious to me, and I want to give him something precious to tell him so."

"Like a diamond?" asked Doc.

"Yes," Snow White replied.

"Don't you worry, Snow White," said Doc. "I'll take care of it myself!"

"Oh, thank you so much," she said.

Grumpy wanted to be the one to find the perfect diamond for Snow White, but he overslept the next morning, and the other Dwarfs had already left!

"Dagnab it!" grumbled Grumpy. He rushed out the door—and ran right into the Prince!

"Well, hello, Grumpy," said the Prince. "I'm glad to find you at home. I have a favor to ask."

"Snow White and I will be celebrating our first anniversary tonight," said the Prince. "Can you help me find a perfect diamond for her?"

"I'll find the most beautiful, most sparklin', most dazzlin' diamond in the whole mine!" Grumpy said proudly.

Deep in the mine, Doc soon found his perfect diamond, and he hurried off to tell the other Dwarfs.

Grumpy was also deep in the mine—and he found the same beautiful diamond! He raced off to get a pickaxe.

Meanwhile, Dopey wandered through the mine alone, looking for the perfect diamond for Snow White—and there it was! It was the diamond Doc and Grumpy had chosen! Carefully, Dopey dislodged the diamond with his pickaxe and then began tapping it with a chisel.

Doc, Grumpy, and the other Dwarfs hurried back to see the perfect diamond. When they got there, they saw Dopey chipping away at it!

"Dopey!" they shouted.

Dopey looked up. His pickaxe slipped and hit the diamond—and the jewel broke into two pieces!

"That was the perfect diamond I found," said Doc. "I was going to give it to Snow White for the Prince."

"You mean that was the perfect diamond *I* found," said Grumpy. "I was goin' to give it to the Prince for Snow White. Now what will we do?"

Doc sighed. "We'll just have to explain."

Grumpy and Doc each put one half of the diamond in a bag. Dopey found some vines to tie the bags shut.

At the Seven Dwarfs' cottage, Snow White had just set the table for two. She couldn't wait for the Dwarfs to return with her gift for the Prince.

The Prince ate his home-cooked meal slowly, enjoying every bite. But he couldn't wait to give Snow White her gift.

Snow White and the Prince were just finishing their pie when the Dwarfs returned. Snow White smiled at Doc. The Prince smiled at Grumpy. Then Doc slowly set his bag in front of Snow White, while Grumpy gave his to the Prince.

Snow White and the Prince looked at each other in surprise.

"This is my present for you," said Snow White as she touched her bag.

The Prince picked up his bag. "We must think alike," he said. "This is for you."

"Oh, darling," said Snow White, opening the bag. "How unusual." She held up the diamond half.

"Yes," said the Prince, disappointed. "Unusual."

Snow White handed the Prince her bag. When he pulled out his broken diamond, she almost cried.

The Prince squeezed Snow White's hand. "It's beautiful, my dear, because it is from you," he said.

Suddenly, Dopey hurried to the table and pointed to the diamonds.

"I'm sorry, Dopey," said the Prince. "We don't understand."

Dopey picked up the two diamond halves. And as the Prince and Snow White watched, he joined the two pieces to form one perfect heart. Snow White and the Prince nodded at Dopey and smiled.

"Happy anniversary," Snow White and the Prince said to each other.

Later that night, the Prince and Snow White danced beneath the twinkling stars—and beside their heart-shaped diamond. It was a wonderful anniversary!

A Moment to Remember

By Catherine McCafferty

$\mathcal{P}$rincess Aurora sighed. Life in the palace was so very different from the quiet glade where she had met Prince Phillip. That night there would be yet another royal ball, and the fairies were arguing over what she should wear.

"Now, dears," said Flora, "we all know that this outfit suits Aurora best. Don't you think so, Aurora?"

Before Aurora could answer them, Prince Phillip came
into the room.

"Hello, dearest," he said.

"Oh, Phillip, I'm so glad to see you. I—" Aurora began.

"Ahem," the royal florist interrupted. "Princess Aurora, could you please tell the royal table setter that she must place flowers in the middle of each table tonight?"

"And could you please tell the royal florist that our guests won't see one another if I put his big flower arrangements on the tables?" said the royal table setter.

"Let's put just one flower on each table," Aurora suggested.

"A single flower?" muttered the servants. "The guests will be insulted!"

"You were saying, dear?" Phillip asked.

"Pardon me, Princess," said the royal steward, "but you must approve the seating arrangements."

"Thank you, Steward," said Aurora. "I will look at them—"

"When we return," Prince Phillip finished. He took the surprised princess's hand. "We're going out where no one can ask us anything."

As they mounted their horses, Phillip turned to Aurora.
"I'm sorry, I forgot that the Royal Guard must come with us."

Aurora looked at the ten riders behind them and tried to hide her disappointment. Then she leaned down and whispered to Phillip's horse. Samson charged away from the palace with Aurora's horse following him. Soon the Royal Guard was far behind.

"Whoa, Samson!" Phillip shouted. But the horse galloped deep into the forest. Then Samson stopped suddenly.

Splash! Phillip sailed over Samson's head and landed in a stream.

"No carrots for you, boy!" Prince Phillip scolded his horse. He looked up and saw Aurora trying to hide a giggle.

"Do you remember this place, Phillip?" Aurora asked.

Phillip climbed out of the stream. He pulled off his boots and dumped the water out of them.

Aurora took off her shoes, too. She spun around gracefully, humming a tune.

"Yes," Prince Phillip said softly. "I remember this place. . . ."

"I will never forget that day," said Aurora, "no matter how crowded our lives become with royal duties."

Prince Phillip smiled. "Nor will I," he told her.

Phillip and Aurora held hands, wishing they could bring the peace and love they knew in the glade back to the palace.

Their peaceful moment ended as the Royal Guard thundered
into the glade.

Phillip put on his hat and cape. Then he handed Aurora
a single flower.

Aurora took the gift and smiled. "We should go back and get
ready for the ball," she said.

"You go ahead, dear," Phillip said. "I'll be back soon."

As she rode off, Aurora decided to plan a special surprise for the prince.

Meanwhile, Phillip had a surprise of his own.

"Not a word of this to the princess," he said to her animal friends as he gathered some flowers.

For the rest of the afternoon, Princess Aurora worked on Phillip's surprise. Flora, Fauna, and Merryweather flitted about, helping wherever they could.

More than once, Aurora heard a servant murmur, "Our guests will certainly be . . . surprised."

Aurora just smiled. "It is Prince Phillip I want to surprise," she said. "Not a word of this to him."

That night, after the fairies had helped Aurora into her gown, Prince Phillip came into the room. He held out a simple crown made from the flowers of the glade. "Would you like to wear this, too?" he asked.

"Oh, Phillip!" Aurora cried as she put on the crown and hugged her husband. "It is perfect for this evening."

Aurora led Phillip down the stairs to the ballroom. "Now I
have a surprise for *you!*" The ballroom was dark and empty.

"You've canceled the ball?" Prince Phillip asked.

"No, Phillip," Aurora answered. "You brought a bit of our little
glade to me in this beautiful crown. Now let me take you back to
our glade."

A sweet breeze blew through the flowers and trees in the ballroom's courtyard. Water danced in the fountain. Candles flickered in the darkness.

"The glade will always be in our hearts," Aurora whispered. "But now it is in our palace, too."

Just then, Phillip's father, King Hubert, approached.

"This is much better than the stuffy balls I usually attend," he said to Princess Aurora. "Thank you, my dear!"

And as Aurora and Phillip danced, their little friends added
their own magic from the glade.